JUST A LITTLE CRUSH

By Willow Winters & Amelia Wilde

I had to convince myself it was just a little flirtation between us.

When I first met her at the bar, she was already taken.

She was my younger sister's friend from college who was moving to our small town after graduation. Smart and beautiful, with a smile that made me feel things I'd never felt before, I was hooked instantly. My pulse would race and I found myself eager to make her laugh, to have her brush against me, even if it was only friendly flirtation. Before I knew it, I turned into some schoolboy with puppy love just at the sight of her.

I thought: this feeling won't last. I shouldn't be thinking about settling down. She's just a passing fascination.

But she kept coming around and that desire never went away.

The timing was never right. We became too close, too good of friends to risk anything.

Neither of us ever crossed a line, and at some point, I started to believe it really was only a harmless little crush.

Until one night, I kissed her …

This is a cute and sexy friends-to-lovers romance. Enjoy!

AUBREE

*E*very Sunday night during football season, a game blares from the corner of the bar. The TV mounted on the wall was updated last year, the pool table is even newer and although the back room and one side of the bar is taken by men with gray beards who have come here for decades, this half of The Peanut Bar and Grill is ours.

It's been ours for three years now, ever since I moved to this small town. The only thing missing is our names carved into the tabletop at our regular booth.

Same crew every Sunday, and on Wednesdays too for half-price nachos. A smile grows on my lips as the bar cheers, someone shouts in protest and Dani, the bartender, breaks out in a laugh. She and I are alike; neither one of us really cares about football, but this is a part of home.

Nick and Michelle, high school sweethearts who have been married for five years now, are cuddled up in the corner of the booth. They'll leave early, just like they have since she found out she's pregnant.

It wasn't even on the menu until Michelle told the owner she was craving them during her first trimester. He's her neighbor and said it's the least he could do.

I take another sip of my pale ale just as the happy couple makes the rounds to say goodbye, root beer float in hand.

Jackson and Nate mock protest over them leaving although every single one of us knew it was going to happen. The other five of us will be here till close most likely.

Nate and his girlfriend, my close friend Anne. The rest of us are the single bunch: Jackson, Cheryl, and me.

"Have twice as much fun for me," Michelle says and sighs sweetly as she gives me a hug, her belly nudging against mine. Her flowy cream blouse peeks out from her jean jacket that wouldn't close around her if she tried. It's not maternity, but it's darn cute.

"Where's your sweater?" Nick questions,

cutting me off in a protective tone that's all too adorable just as she's snatching it from the seat with a smirk on her face. It's cute how he is with her, and just as cute how she toys with him.

His smirk matches hers once she gives him a peck on the lips.

I can't help but feel a pang of jealousy watching the two of them wave as they exit the bar. Hand in hand. Madly in love.

Another sip of my beer heats my cheeks as I peek at Jackson. Nick and Michelle had one side of the booth. Nate and Anne, the other. Then Cheryl and I took the outside seats while Jackson, Cheryl's older brother, sat at the barstool closest to the table.

That's been our setup for years.

Three years of sitting just feet away from a man I have a crush on, every single week. Ever since I moved to this small town.

"Another?" Dani calls out, catching my attention. Her dark eyes stare back at me and it's only then that I look down and realize my glass is nearly empty.

"Yeah," I answer and the tall brunette is already pouring me another. She works this side of the room. Her brother works the other. The Peanut Bar is a family place. Practically everything in this town is that way.

It's all close quarters and routines. Everyone knows everyone and also their business.

Which is why my fingers fiddle with my drink a moment too long before I nudge Jackson, opting to hand him the empty glass, which he easily exchanges for the full one Dani's holding out to him to pass to me.

My heart does a little pitter-patter every time he looks my way. His sharp blue eyes and charming smile aren't what gets me, although they don't hurt. There's something else about him. And when his fingers brush against mine, in that small moment of contact, a heat blazes through me.

For three years it's been like this. And every day that passes without acknowledging what he does to me, only makes it harder the next.

The bar cheers again as the screen shows a play-back of the game. Cheryl's busy chatting with Nate and Anne. The couple behind us, neighbors of Cheryl, leans over the back of their booth to join the conversation.

I stare up at the screen, pretending I don't want to glance back at Jackson, pretending I don't wish he was sitting next to me and the whole damn town knew we were a thing.

Jackson's my friend, tall, dark and handsome … but *only* a friend.

The timing was simply never right for us to be

anything more.

When I met him, the butterflies were there, the instant attraction undeniable … but I tried to deny it, because I had a boyfriend. It was a long-distance situation—I'd graduated college and left that town to come here, but I was determined to make it work. Cheryl, my friend from college who convinced me to move here, introduced me to her brother and it was damn hard to keep my impression of him to myself.

Jackson greeted me with a charming smile and a laugh that made me feel things it shouldn't have. After three years of this charade, Cheryl is well aware I have a crush on her brother.

I wasn't the first of her friends to feel puppy love for him. Apart from some teasing here and there, she's kept that information to herself and we remain the closest of friends.

Thank God. I love her like family, and I don't know what I would do without her. Without any of them really. She became the sister I never had while we were in college. As far as I'm concerned, this town and these people adopted me.

Which is why I'll never cross that line with Jackson.

Back then, when she first introduced us, I thought: he's not into me like that, and he's not going to be hanging out with us all the time anyway.

So I need to get the idea of the two of us out of my head.

Only he did keep coming around, and those feelings kept growing. I didn't realize just how tight knit this town is.

Over the following months, I realized I couldn't deny what I felt. So I did the right thing, I ended the three-month relationship I had so I could confess to Jackson how I felt. But when I went to the bar, in that spot across from me, right where Jackson is sitting now, there was a cute little redhead by the name of Mallory attached to his hip. And she made him smile, so I couldn't hate her.

Back and forth for years, one of us was always taken. I'd convinced myself it was meant to be that way because as time went on, he became my rock for so many things. Just like Cheryl.

"You want a root beer float?" a masculine voice murmurs close to the shell of my ear. My body heats with a flush that I'm sure is visible. And that baritone cadence elicits an ache of desire between my thighs.

He knows exactly what he's doing. The cocky grin on his handsome face tells me so as he stands back upright, a hand on the back of the booth. He towers over me in blue jeans and a simple plaid button-down.

"We could get one with beer and ice cream?"

Jackson offers, lifting his glass in mock cheers before taking a sip. The bar erupts as our team scores, yet the noise seems to fade and blur behind him. Even with the scent of beer in the air, I know exactly how he smells. It's like amber and woods, mixed with a hint of freshness.

Instead of saying anything at all that's on my mind, I answer as I should, in a teasing, nonserious manner. "You want beer with ice cream?" I shake my head gently, a crease between my furrowed brow as I add, "What is wrong with you?"

He lets out a laugh and motions for me to slide down the booth so he can sit next to me.

The leather is still warm from where Michelle was sitting as I scoot back. It's quiet back here, slightly more private but not really.

"So you don't want to split ice cream with me?" he questions, a touch of his Southern drawl coming through, along with feigned vulnerability in his puppy dog eyes.

Yes. Jackson knows exactly what he's doing when he flirts with me.

And I know what I'm doing when I flirt back. "If by 'split' you mean I get a whole three bites before you devour it, then sure." I shrug and pull a leg up onto the seat so I can wrap my arm around it. My black leggings and baggy gray knit sweater keep my appearance casual. Although I did spend time on my makeup, keeping it relatively natural but with a hint of pink. Heavy mascara and a braid down my left shoulder were the finishing touches.

His hand runs down the side of his chiseled, stubbled jaw as he chuckles. "I asked you last time we split a dessert if you wanted more," he protests. Leaning closer he adds, "If I knew you were going to hold it against me, I wouldn't have touched your half." He's close enough now that I can feel his heat, I can smell him too and it's just like I knew it would be.

Before I can answer, a balled-up napkin hits Jackson square on his nose. "Get a room," a grinning Cheryl calls out from across the booth. Nate and Anne are laughing, and the couple behind them in the booth adjacent to ours is laughing too. Not at us, thankfully. They don't seem to notice and with a smile, Cheryl's already left the table. With a bit of a tipsy sway, she's headed to the bar before either Jackson or I can answer.

Thump, *thump*, my heart batters against my rib cage in protest, but this tension doesn't affect Jackson in the least. He's never bothered and I know it's because he doesn't feel what I feel.

He doesn't feel this pull between us like I do.

My throat's dry and I try to swallow down my nerves with a sip of the cool beer as Jackson leaves my side, the leather groaning as he goes.

JACKSON

"*Y*ou should just go for it, man," Nate comments, sidling up beside me at the bar as Dani puts in the order.

"And you should mind your own damn business," I joke back at him, pretending like Aubree doesn't get to me. Like I don't want to slide in next to her and press my lips against hers. I have to hold back a groan at the thought. I'm not a lightweight, but four lagers and apparently I'm feeling the effects.

"I think you two should just get together for a night. Just saying it might be good to finally clear that sexual tension."

My body reacts to the suggestion, but so does the last sober bit of me. "And ruin our friendship?"

Nate's smirk and lifted brow piss me off. "Don't

act like it's not a possibility," I tell him lowly, leaning against the bar top, hoping he gets it. He's been joking about it for months since he caught me staring at her like some lovesick puppy dog. "If we did anything, you know damn well it would change everything between us."

Nate's dark eyes narrow as he seems to consider my dilemma. It's only ever been a joke. Nothing like the conversation we're having now and how I'm riddled with anxiousness.

"How would you feel if some guy came in and they started making out?" he asks and as he does, I set my glass down a little too hard on the bar top. It doesn't crack, but the sound is jarring enough that Dani turns from the tap, her brow raised.

I raise a hand in defense and say, "Didn't break it. Sorry."

"No harm, no foul," she answers with a grin.

"Come on, how would you feel," Nate presses, dropping his voice so no one can hear. Honestly, I'm not sure if they can or not in this crowd. I'm tipsy and the bar is loud, but in this small town everyone seems to hear everything even when it's whispered. "If some guy came in, hit on her and they hit it off." He gestures behind us. "If they were making out in that booth you were just sitting in beside her."

"She wouldn't do that." My head shakes and my

entire body stiffens. I never knew jealousy until Aubree introduced me to her boyfriend years ago. I'm not a fan.

"If it happened, you wouldn't like that."

"I'd be happy that she's happy." I give him the lie and take refuge in my beer. It's crisp and cold still, even though it's the last of it.

"Bullshit," Nate says, not letting up.

Squaring my shoulders, I stare him down. "Let it go, man."

Every other reason gets caught in my throat:

If she was into me, I'd know by now.

If it was going to happen, it would have happened by now.

Nate shrugs, the jersey he's wearing pulling tighter on his shoulders. "Fine," he states casually, but then adds, "Don't come crying to me when some other guy is the one to get cozy with her 'cause you don't have the balls to kiss her first."

I'm paralyzed with a mix of emotions. I don't trust myself to answer. Nate seems to notice my lack of a response and glances over my way.

"Fuck, man, I'm sorry. Just ignore me. All right?"

Anger bristles along my shoulders as I turn to face the TV in the corner, although it also allows me to watch Aubree from the corner of my eye.

"I mean it, I'm sorry. I just … think you two would hit it off."

My tongue sweeps along my bottom lip as I watch Aubree finish her beer. Her cheeks are flushed, her hair's in a loose braid and a smile graces her face from whatever my sister just told her.

"I just can't risk changing some things, you know?" I say, finally answering Nate.

"They're going to change either way," he tells me in all seriousness and there's an ache in my chest. A familiar pull like the sense of loss. Loss of something I've never even had.

The moment Aubree scoots from the booth, her hand reaches out to me as she stabilizes herself, fixing her baggy sweater that swallows up her small frame. It's these little touches that get me.

How she knows she can rely on me. How she likes to even.

"You all good?" I ask her and she lets out a small laugh. That sound. It wriggles its way through me, warming me. Her hazel eyes slip to mine and she bites down slightly on her lower lip. "Just have to run to the ladies' room."

"You might want to walk, it's a bit crowded," I tease her. It's cheesy and the grin Nate has growing on his face tells me he heard it too.

Whatever, she still laughs.

Shaking her head, she brushes past me, and everything inside of me wants to wrap my arm around her waist, pull her in and ask her if she wants to come home with me.

It's a feeling I'm used to. And so is this chill that sweeps in the moment she walks away.

"Dani, she needs another," I call out to the bartender the moment Aubree's gone.

Dani's quick to place the beer down in front of me even though it's for Aubree.

"She didn't even ask who 'she' is," Nate comments.

Reaching over the tabletop, I snag an orange slice Dani forgot, and drop it into Aubree's glass. "Can't I be happy with this as it is?" I ask him genuinely.

Before he can answer, Aubree's right there, watching me place the beer at her seat.

"You looking out for me? Or just trying to get me drunk?" There's this small smile she gives me sometimes. It's there now as she lifts the beer to her lips and slips deeper into the booth to give me room to sit if I want to.

"Maybe a little of both," I joke, questioning if I should sit. If I should push it a little more tonight than I have before.

"Which one would you prefer?" I ask her,

feeling this hot nervousness prick along every inch
of my skin as she stares up at me.

   She smirks back, all flirtatious and never
breaking eye contact when she says, "Maybe a little
of both?"

AUBREE

*C*heryl leans in close, a smirk clearly written on her face. "Just do it, Bree." She comes even closer to nudge me, her tipsiness making her sway as she adds, "You can't keep teasing him like this."

The grin on her face is as wide as it can be as her gaze lifts from me and moves to the topic of the conversation behind me.

My cheeks can't get any hotter.

"Your drink's empty." A deep yet flirtatious man's voice reaches us from down the bar. *Kill me now.* Cheryl and I grabbed barstools beside Nate and Jackson when the game went into overtime. Both of them have since moved. It's like musical chairs in this place.

It took a whole two minutes for the guys to my

right to start chatting us up. They weren't paying attention to the game in the least.

"Let us buy you your next round. What are you ladies drinking?"

He raises his voice to speak over the sounds of the game on the bar's TVs. The crowd roars in the background. Whistles blow. I don't care much about the score, but the atmosphere is amped up. The end of the night is getting close.

Cheryl beams at me. "See? If you don't make your move, somebody else is going to step in. Those guys are hot."

"Those guys are hot because you're drunk," I joke, although I don't have much room to talk. I, too, am far from sober.

"No, they're genuinely hot." Cheryl sneaks a peek over her shoulder, her cheeks turning a bright pink as she takes them in.

The bar is emptying out. Quite a few people reached their limit by the fourth quarter and headed home, but Cheryl's having a good time. Nate and Anne made it through most of the fourth before they went home to make out with each other.

And Jackson …

Jackson is still here.

I can feel him in the bar. Maybe it's just because I'm drunk as well, but I am acutely aware he's still here, even with my back turned. He's behind me now at the booth I was sitting at only an hour or so ago.

I wonder if he's watching. If those guys come closer, he's going to see. The Peanut Bar isn't that big, and there aren't many people left. Nerves eat at me as I wonder if he even cares. All I can think about while these guys are flirting with me, is whether or not Jackson can see. What the hell is wrong with me?

With a short sigh, I push my beer away and look back at my good friend. Her teeth are sunken into her bottom lip as she glances their way again.

Cheryl's right. I should make a move, one way or the other. Three years is a long time to shove my feelings down. Three years is a long time not to go home with a man because of a little crush that's never going to go anywhere. I should either get up and confess to Jackson that my heart skips a beat every time I see him here, or I should let those guys buy us drinks.

The moment I suck in a breath and peek at Jackson, I turn right back around.

It's silly to be afraid of rejection like this, but I am. If he outright turned me down, it would hurt like hell. And then I could never show my face again at this bar. Never ever. This place is like a second home to me.

"Pale ale," I call to the guys down the bar. The

one closest to me nods and I shrug, offering a smile. "That's what I'm having, anyway." He's cute. Handsome even, although the jersey makes him seem a little young. He's definitely in college, and old enough to be in a bar so I'm thinking twenty-two maybe.

"I'm tempted to ask him if he's going to be a dentist because his teeth are freaking perfect," I comment to Cheryl and she pats my arm a little too hard.

"Hell yes," she says, a little too loud. "Now we're going to have some fun. Or at least you are." She gets up from her stool, the legs scraping against the wooden floor as if she's leaving me. The urge to grab her arm and cling to her has never been stronger.

"What?" The one word that spills out of my mouth sounds utterly pathetic and I don't even care. "You are not leaving me," I whisper in a hushed voice.

"I'm just going to the restroom. You get the first pick of the guys."

"Cheryl!" I reach for her sleeve, but she's already too far to pull her back.

The two guys don't miss a beat sliding down farther, like they're coming in for the kill.

"So, a pale ale?" the blond with the gorgeous smile questions and then motions for Dani. I don't miss how high her brow arches and that sly, comical smile she gives me.

"Mm-hm." I don't trust myself to speak, but I settle on some small talk.

"Hi, guys. Having a good night so far?"

"Depends," the blond one says. "Are you?"

My cheeks flare with heat. He's not subtle in the least but I play it casually. "I always have fun on Sunday nights."

The truth is, I'm always invested in being here on Sunday nights. Our crew has a good time together and it's my wind down time. My safe place. But I'd be lying if I said I wasn't here for Jackson too. My smile slips as I think of him yet again. I like being around him. I like having an excuse to look at him and listen to his jokes and just be in the same room. I've had to come to terms with making the most of it and enjoying my Sundays over the last three years. If it was truly painful to be here with him, that wouldn't be any fun.

The barstool scrapes as the blond hunk takes the stool next to mine, the one that used to be Cheryl's, and purses his lips. "You could have more fun, I bet." His tone is soothing, but I see through it all.

"Oh yeah? And how's that?" If I wasn't thinking of Jackson, I'd ask him if he wanted to cut to the chase.

As it is, even when I'm looking at this man

who's obviously interested in me, all I see is the image of Jackson sitting here only hours ago.

My heart's beating faster, but I don't know if it's because I'm genuinely interested in this guy or because I'm nervous as hell about what's going to happen. If I click with some random man at the bar, what happens to my feelings about Jackson? Probably nothing. He doesn't have any for me, so we'd both move on with our lives like grown adults. All the while this guy talks, my thoughts scream in my head. I nod and comment when it seems appropriate. His friend hovers, more invested in the game now.

But damn if I don't want Jackson to be jealous. At least for him to notice that someone else has approached me. It sends a shiver down my spine to imagine his eyes on us, but I don't look to see if he's watching.

"What are you doing after this?" the blond hunk questions. My lips part but someone else speaks before I can.

"We're going to my place." Jackson's deep, masculine voice breaks into our conversation and heats my core.

My heart pounds and I let out a long breath. It's so damn hot in here. I hadn't noticed that before. I pull at my sweater, hoping to feel a little breeze.

Before I can say anything, shock and heat overwhelming me, Jackson's strong arm wraps around my lower waist. The thermostat must have fucking broken in this place.

Jackson's body curls around mine as he bends down and kisses the crook of my neck. Right there in that spot beneath my ear and I think I must have died. It's heaven, it's sinful. It's a fantasy come to life. "That's what she's doing after this." His chest is a deep rumble against my shoulder and I can barely look back at the man who just bought me a drink.

I don't even know how I'm sitting upright.

The brush of his lips fills me with butterflies. A fluttering mess of them. Gulping down the beer, I give myself a moment to steady. Jackson. Possessive of me in the bar just because a guy offered me a drink?

This might be my only shot to play along with him. I turn my face to his and kiss his cheek before I can overthink this. If he's going to cross this line for a joke or whatever Jackson's thinking ... I'm going to cross it too.

My blond would-be hero throws his hands up with a smile when I glance back at him. "Didn't realize."

"Sorry, I should have said—" I'm not able to finish before Jackson cuts me off.

"No problem." His tone is familiar, yet harder,

more dominating. He leaves no room for further conversation. And the other guys get the hint.

They back off, looking toward the hall leading to the restroom, leaving me staring up at him, his arm still wrapped around me. His hold is looser now, but it's still there.

"You drunk?" he questions, glancing down at me for only a moment.

Maybe more than a little tipsy. "Not so drunk that I don't know what I want." The words slip out before I can stop them and his brow raises in surprise.

I rip my gaze away and take another sip of beer, but it doesn't do anything to change the way I feel right now.

I've never been hornier in my life. I didn't come here with sex on my mind. I'm in leggings and a sweater. That should be enough of a clue that I didn't plan on doing anything but cuddling up with a hangover cure after this.

Jackson says something and I'm not quite sure what, but his hand leaves the bar and I'll be damned if I'm going to let him leave me like this.

"What was that?" I question, my voice sultry. I didn't mean for it to come out like that.

"Just cockblocking you," Jackson jokes. He picks up his drink from the bar behind me. That hammering in my chest intensifies. Is he … is he toying with me? 'Cause that kiss is still burning my neck.

"Oh yeah? What would you call this?" I say, then lean forward, hook my arm around his neck, and kiss him full on the mouth. My lips press against his and at first they're hard, but they mold to mine instantly.

He kisses me back with an intensity I didn't expect. He tastes like beer and hunger. He tastes better than I ever imagined he would. I kiss him deeper, wanting to remember it after tonight.

That's when it hits me. We're in the freaking bar still. Everyone is here. His sister. Our friends. I pull away with a slight panic.

Jackson smirks down at me. A gorgeous, handsome, and somewhat cocky smirk. It's a look that keeps me calm while everything else blurs around us.

I almost ask him if he wants to get out of here, but the words fall short. My heart stops with the fear that he'll reject me. Tell me it was all in fun, and it's not like that. I'm just a friend of his sister. I just wanted those guys to back off. That's what he'll say.

In my short moment of fear, Jackson pushes a stray lock of my hair back and leans in again for a gentle, yet demanding kiss.

This time, he flicks his tongue against my lips

until I part them for him. Inwardly I sigh with relief. It's been three years of waiting, and honestly, I thought it would be a lifetime. I never thought Jackson would kiss me at all and especially not like this. He's tasting me like I tasted him. I swear, he wants me too.

He lets out a groan against my mouth. "You want to get out of here?"

JACKSON

There's no going back.

That's all I can think as my hands roam down her soft curves in the back of the car. Her lips haven't left mine and if I thought that this may not be the only chance I have with Aubree, I'd contain myself. I'd show a semblance of control, but as it stands, I have none.

There is nothing but desperation for her not to stop. To just let me kiss her.

Soft moans pour from her lips, subtle and just as desperate as my touch. The Uber slows to a stop and I barely look up, checking for a red light or a stop sign. Instead I see my front lawn.

I pull my lips from hers, but intertwine our fingers and keep her close. "Let's go," I tell her. Tomorrow is vaguely on my mind. The questions and concerns. Every time a thought pierces through the haze of lust, I shut it down by kissing her again.

As we climb out, Aubree kisses my neck in that tender spot above my shoulder and it only makes my dick harder. The simple act elicits a groan from me and the moment I close the car door, I lift Aubree into my arms.

With a gasp of surprise and delight, she wraps her legs around my hips. One of my arms supports her from under her ass, the other braces her back and keeps her close to me. Her lips find mine again and I swear to God I'm in heaven.

The scent of her hair around me, the feel of her warmth against me.

I want more. I need more.

It's dark inside when I unlock the door and kick it open. It's not as smooth of a transition as I'd like it to be, but I'm able to do it all while kissing her. Little nips of her bottom lip and the sweet heated gasps she gives me have me impossibly hard.

My front door bangs recklessly against the wall, and I don't give a fuck.

"Make sure it's locked," she whispers and I have to chuckle.

"Yes, ma'am," I comment as I set her down gently, for the first time letting her go. She flicks on the corner light of the living room. She's been here a thousand times before, but never just the two of us. With the click of the lock, I look over to see her standing in the middle of the living room, looking so out of place as she stares back at me. Her wide hazel eyes are filled with lust and desire.

As if knowing I've dreamed of this moment, she crosses her arms in front of her and slowly pulls the sweater over her head, letting it drop to the floor into a puddle of fabric beside her.

I can barely breathe, paralyzed by the sight of her stripping. The wooden floor creaks as I take a single step toward her. She sinks her teeth into her bottom lip, her cheeks flushed as she unhooks her bra, letting it fall to the floor. I take another step forward and another, so very aware of what's about to happen.

There's no going back.

Vulnerability shines in her hazel eyes as she looks back at me, but she doesn't stop. As her thumbs hook into the top of her leggings, I place my hands over hers and lower my lips to the shell of her ear to whisper, "Let me."

Her head falls back slightly as she murmurs her agreement. My lips travel down her body, leaving openmouthed kisses as I go. I take my time to pluck her hardened nipples and smile against her heated skin when she moans from the touch.

From what I do to her.

Groaning against her curves, I nip along her

body as I lower myself to my knees. As I tug her leggings down, I pull her lace underwear along with it.

Her fingers spear through my hair the moment I peek up at her. She's bared to me and I lean forward, tasting her. Her eyes flutter as her head falls back and with that I take a languid lick and then another. Her arousal is sweet on my tongue.

Both of her hands brace against my shoulders as she struggles to stay upright when I suck her clit. I massage my tongue against her and my sweet Aubree digs her nails into my shoulders, sucks in a breath and then calls out my name.

My name.

My hands dig into her ass to keep her where I want her. Precum leaks from my cock as she writhes, the leggings still wrapped around her ankles, preventing her from moving much at all.

"Please," she begs me and I can't take it anymore.

In a swift motion I lift her up, stepping on the leggings to rip them from her and hustle to the sofa. I'm not as gentle as I'd like to be when I lay her down.

She gasps from the sudden change of pace.

My shirt comes over my head, and I kick my jeans off as quickly as possible. All the while the sofa protests under us.

"Spread your legs for me," I murmur and she obeys, her wide eyes staying on mine. Without wasting a second, I slam into her.

Her wet, welcoming heat takes me like she's meant to. Her lips part in a gorgeous *O* and she holds her breath as I push myself deeper, rocking slightly so my groin massages her clit.

"You're so fucking tight," I groan and then lower myself down to her, bracing a forearm beside her so I can kiss her.

It's only then that I move. Pulling nearly all the way out before pushing all the way back in. The head of my cock presses against her back wall and I can barely take it.

"Jackson." She moans my name, her arms wrapping around my back. Her head thrashes from side to side as I push myself in deeper and fuck her harder with each thrust.

There's a moment when her hands brush against my chest, with her chest rising and falling with each heavy breath, that our eyes meet. My heart hammers, my blood heats and I swear she almost says what I'm thinking.

Instead she kisses me, pressing her lips to mine as if she would die without it.

I go slow for a moment, wanting it back. Wanting that moment back and needing to know what she was going to say.

The three words are right there for me too, but I swallow them down and lower my chest to hers, holding her as I fuck her faster, but deeper still.

"Fuck!" she yelps and her pussy flutters around my cock. My thumb finds her clit and a cold sweat forms on my back as it all intensifies.

Her muffled cries of pleasure fill the room and I fucking love it. I've always wanted her, I've fantasized about it, but this? The sight of her getting off on my cock is better than I could have imagined.

"Jackson." She calls out my name again, this time with desperation as I hook my arm under her knee and pull it up so I can get even deeper.

"Don't worry," I say and kiss her neck. "You can take me." With that whispered, I piston my hips, fucking her deeply and roughly.

She comes again, screaming my name this time and I can't stop. I take her savagely. Without holding back a damn thing and I don't come until she reaches her third climax.

AUBREE

*I*t's all slow and fuzzy when I first wake up, which isn't uncommon for the morning after a Sunday night out. It all depends on how the game goes. If it's a close one, with lots of tension and shouting, I can still feel it in my muscles the day after. But something is off. I know it even before I'm aware I'm unfortunately hungover.

It's not the lingering effects of too many shots that's making me feel heavy and sated, though.

Since when did my blankets have this much weight to them?

It only takes one weak stretch to feel another person under the sheets. With wide eyes and a quick glance around Jackson's living room, all of last night tumbles into my memory.

Oh, no, no, no, no, no, no, no.

It comes back all at once, and the shock feels like a shot glass slamming down on the bar. Jackson. *I came home with Jackson last night.*

It's futile to pull the sheet up against my bare chest as I stare down at his naked form. How the hell did we both sleep on his couch?

I did more than *sleep* on this sofa.

The cushion groans slightly and I slow my movements as I attempt to slip out, still very much naked and groggy.

Every little moment flashes back and the conflicting emotions intensify. He kissed the side of my neck in front of the entire bar. He upped the ante in the game we played for years. Was he jealous of the guys who were hitting on me? Or … I don't know. All I know is that it became something else when I kissed him back.

I barely remember anything about the ride home. All I remember is his mouth on mine, the deep murmurs and lust-filled groans. And how warm his body felt against mine.

Last night was better than I ever imagined it would be. The morning after, though? Well, there's a reason I've never dreamed of this moment.

Bottom line: we crossed a big red line last night in front of everyone. That truth is a flashing bright light in my face as I tiptoe across the living room in search of my underwear.

Sex with your best friend's brother is a no-no. I can already see the look of shock on Cheryl's face. I can already imagine how awkward our group outings with friends will be.

Blood drains from my face and the regret slips in.

I never meant to take it this far.

My heart pounds as I stand paralyzed, clinging to Jackson's navy blue comforter which is pressed against my chest. His living room is neat and masculine in the pale early morning sun filtering through the blinds. Apart from our clothes from last night strewn across the carpeted floor.

Eventually, I take in Jackson's sleeping form. His firm—and bare—ass is fully on display, his arm hanging over the edge of the sofa. He's dead to the world and guiltily I lay the comforter across him. His face is turned toward the back of the sofa, and his other arm is tucked under his pillow in a way that shows off his muscular frame. Broad shoulders rise and fall with every deep breath. Just as I feel a touch of ease, he mumbles something I can barely hear and I freeze. A beat passes and then another.

All the while, the slight chill in the room skims across my nakedness.

Clothes. For the love of all things holy. Where are my clothes?

It doesn't take long to spot them, but each quiet moment comes with a hint of regret.

Why does Cheryl have to have the hottest brother in the history of the world? It's not fair. That's what I've told myself for so long now. It's not fair, because I can never be with him.

Except I have been with him. We were together last night. He wanted me to come home with him, and I said yes, and now …

Now I have to get out of here.

Part of me wants to touch his shoulder, wake him up, and give him a repeat performance. To fake it until we make it, so to speak.

A big part of me, actually. Most of me. I want to feel his body against mine again. He was powerful and confident over me in a way that no other man has been. At the same time, he was familiar. Safe. Jackson knows me really well, and for good reason. We've been friends for years.

Oh, Aubree, what have you done?

The reality, though, is that I have morning breath, bed head, a hangover and regrets a mile long, as well as a growing list of insecurities and uncertainties. So the only faking I'll be doing is faking that everything is okay until I am safely home and clinging to my own pillow.

I silently gather each garment like I've been trained by the CIA in extraction methods.

My purse dangles from one corner of the coffee table. The garments scattered around the room tell a definite story about what happened last night. Two people couldn't get enough of each other, and they couldn't even aim for the furniture when they took their clothes off.

Not that I need the clothes to tell me anything. I remember how amazing it felt to be in Jackson's arms. I remember how much I wanted him. Kissing him woke something up in me. Something that's been bubbling under the surface for way too long.

I step into my clothes quickly and quietly, then snatch my phone up from the ground. There's a text from Cheryl. It's from last night, about half an hour after I left the bar with Jackson.

Cheryl: You did it!! Good for you!! Which of the guys did you go home with?

I text her back with trembling hands. My pulse races as I press send.

Aubree: Don't hate me. Jackson. I'm at Jackson's house. I spent the night here. I'm never going to be able to look him in the eye again.

Never mind that I'll have to look Cheryl in the eye. She'll know I slept with her brother. She did egg me on, but it was a joke. It was all supposed to be harmless fun. My stomach does a nervous flip. I won't be able to stand it if he walks out here all hot and handsome and plays it off like a joke.

Like it didn't mean anything. With both hands running down my face, I wish I could just get in my car and drive away. My fingers fly across my phone ordering my escape car.

My heart pounds as I glance over my shoulder back at Jackson. I don't think I'd be able to play it cool if he sauntered out and pretended it meant nothing.

I can see things going both ways. Next Sunday could be stiff, with us walking on eggshells and all our friends wondering what's going on. Or it could be normal, with both of us pretending to be comfortable. Like it was just a part of the flirtatious game we play.

Or maybe …

Maybe we could be holding hands at the bar. Maybe Jackson could be there as my real boyfriend and not just a decoy for the men who wanted to buy me a drink.

The phone buzzes in my hand and I clutch it to my chest, listening hard for any sign he's waking up. One beat passes and then another of me staring at him like a weirdo.

Without any sign he's woken up, I check my phone.

Cheryl: It was just one night. No big deal. You guys got it out of your system ;)

Out of my system. I swallow thickly.

Reality crashes down around me. Not a soul knows about the crush. The genuine feelings I have for him. No one is going to understand and nothing is going to be all right.

What was I thinking? This isn't the start of a new relationship. This was a one-night stand. In fact, it was a mistake.

My throat tightens. That's exactly what Jackson will say. It was a mistake for the two of us to jump into bed together. Our friendship is too important to screw it up with emotions.

What a mess.

The only way to begin cleaning it up is to leave before he gets out of bed. As if on cue, my phone informs me the getaway car is approaching. It's a little cowardly, I know, to run away after a one-night stand. But if that's all it is, then it won't be anything new. That's what you do when things aren't serious. You go back to your life before they get serious.

I hesitate at the door, my stomach sinking. He might worry about me when he wakes up.

Maybe I should leave a note. I half turn back to the kitchen, but stop myself.

What would the note say?

I had a nice time last night—see you at football!!

Or …

We should talk about this soon so it's not awkward.

Or …

No hard feelings, whatever happens.

Each idea I have is worse than the last. *Shit.* It's better if I don't say anything. It's best if I don't look back. It's better if I chalk it up to a tipsy mistake and leave it in the past where it belongs.

The future with Jackson has to do with friendship. Because we're friends. Really good friends. And that's all we're going to be.

JACKSON

The thud of the front door is far too soft to be what woke me up. If I had to guess, I'd say it's the pounding in my head from a vicious hangover that did it.

With a foggy mind and a heavy body, I lift myself up before realizing what happened.

Aubree. Holy shit, did that really happen last night?

It only takes a moment of listening to the silence in this empty place before I hear a car door shut out front. *Fuck!*

I'm sober in seconds, jolting from the sofa and running toward the door although I don't get far. My foot bashes the coffee table and I seethe, sucking in a deep breath and wincing from the pain.

"Aubree!" I call out as if she could possibly

hear me. By the time I get to the door, I realize I'm completely nude and can't open the door more than a few inches.

The bright morning light blinds me for a moment as I watch the four-door sedan head down the suburban street. Taking Aubree with it and leaving a sense of dread to creep in.

Shit, shit, shit. Running a hand through my hair, I search for a note or for anything at all.

Last night comes back in waves. The drinks, the kissing, fucking Nate texting his friends to flirt with Aubree. I know it was him, trying to prove a point and yeah, he was right.

Seeing her with them … I lean against the wall with my bare ass pressed against the cold surface and regret swarms me.

Last night, I crossed a line, but she crossed it with me. That's the only hope I have, so I hold on to it. Even though she snuck out. Even though there's no note.

I'm quick to find my boxers, putting them on and then searching for my phone in the pocket of the jeans I wore last night.

It's dead … great. Of course it is.

Letting out a sigh, I resign myself to coffee, an Advil and giving myself a moment while the charger brings it back to life.

As the coffee maker sputters and hisses, I

remember how she kissed me. The passion and the desperation. A groan leaves me and my head falls back as my dick remembers last night too.

You can't fake that. She wants me. Or at least she did last night. And it was fucking incredible.

An asymmetric smile pulls my lips up as I add sugar and creamer to my cup and then stir it, the spoon tinking against the ceramic.

Suddenly, the hangover isn't so bad. My pinky toe that's stubbed? Not a big deal. The smile lingers until I check my phone, when it promptly vanishes.

Three texts wait for me, and not a single one from Aubree. My heart sinks further down with each.

Nick: I heard you left the bar with Aubree ... what's going on there?

Nate: So you guys do it?

It's the last one that leaves me wishing Aubree hadn't run off this morning. It's from my sister: **FYI she's freaking out a little. You might want to let her know your friendship is still intact.**

The phone clatters to the counter as I run my hand down the back of my head, cursing myself for taking her home last night. I should have kissed her and told her I wanted to see her. I should have said one damn thought I've had for years about her rather than keeping it to myself.

My phone pings again and although I know it's not her, I wish it were. It's only my sister, asking if I even remember last night because the town is now being informed one text at a time.

Fuck, fuck, everyone knows and I have no idea what it means for us. Panic is something I'm not used to. Not at all when it comes to Aubree. But it's all that takes over until I shove it down.

I've wanted Aubree for so long and now I'm afraid I'm going to lose her ... but I'll be damned if I let that happen.

AUBREE

*A*t least I don't have to go to an office building. That's one small consolation as I stare at my phone wishing a message would pop up. None do, but I count my blessings on the Uber ride back to my apartment, which is on the second floor of a neat brick building with a hair salon on the ground floor and a couple more units up above. I don't mind the muffled sounds of the dryers and music coming through the floor. It's still quiet when I shut the door and lock it behind me with an exacerbated sigh. Not early enough for the first clients of the day.

Thank God I don't have a set schedule, because I desperately need a shower. There's no way I can sit at my desk and go to work while I'm wearing clothes that smell like Jackson.

Maybe it's pathetic, but I can admit it makes me a bit somber to take them off and drop them in the hamper.

I go through all the motions. Shampoo and soap and conditioner. I dry my hair and put on makeup.

Unsurprisingly, it doesn't help. With a hot cup of tea at my side, I take my seat at my computer with a long to-do list and a mind that's full of Jackson. And what we did last night. And how I left him sleeping on the sofa. And how I wish I were still with him. I should have pretended to be sleeping for as long as it took.

In my defense, I'm not good with hangovers.

Graphic design has nothing to do with the man I slept with last night. For fifteen whole minutes, I concentrate on my projects. A new logo for a company based in the city. A banner for an artist's website. The background for a set of wedding invitations.

None of them are exactly presentable … but I try.

All of it takes way longer than it should, because I can't focus.

The only thing that draws my attention is my phone. Every two minutes, I stare at it, willing it to ping and let me know Jackson texted me to tell me how much he wants a repeat of last night.

After about an hour, I find the tea cold and my thoughts turning on me.

I don't know what's worse. If Jackson texts or if he doesn't. If he ignores what happened last night, then I guess that's something to go on. If he texts and wants to talk …

Butterflies flutter deep in my stomach. It's hard to tell if they're the nervous kind or the excited kind.

Of course, there's always the third option, which is that he texts and says we should pretend it didn't happen and was a mistake.

I fly out of my seat so fast the office chair nearly hits the wall as it rolls backward and I put my phone on the kitchen counter, plugging it in to charge. After that, I buckle down for a solid hour of work. There's not a chance in hell I'm going to miss a deadline and get laid off because I let my crush tear up my heart.

It doesn't take long, though, for it to buzz from all the way across the apartment and I'm out of my seat before I can think twice. It's silly to run across my little apartment just for a notification that could be a text from anyone, but I do.

Jackson: You ran off this morning. I should have at least made you breakfast.

Not even one emoji.

How am I supposed to answer this? How am I

supposed to respond? I guess I'll have to play it off like I'm fine and absolutely not obsessed with the outcome of sleeping with my best friend's brother.

Aubree: Sorry—I just didn't want to be late for work!

I sent the exclamation mark before I can think twice. Damn it, I should have changed that to a period.

The typing indicator dots appear on my screen and hover there for what seems like forever. He could say anything right now.

Option A: Let's forget about it. See you Sunday.

Option B: We shouldn't say anything about this. Keep it between us.

No, I correct my thinking, it's too late for that. Cheryl saw. She knows we left together. Everyone who was still at the bar knows. And even if they didn't, there's no way we're pretending it didn't happen.

Jackson: Let me buy you dinner tonight?

My heart's racing slows up slightly, hope in sight. I send a message back without thinking.

Aubree: You don't owe me food just because we had sex :)

I mean it as a joke, but no new dots come up on the screen.

Jackson doesn't say anything.

Not right away. And not in the next hour. Or the hour after that.

The afternoon crawls by. It's the slowest day I've ever lived through. I leave my phone in the kitchen and force myself to work on my projects. This is not a good productivity hack, but it does mean my list gets smaller and smaller as the minutes pass. I answer emails I should have responded to a month ago and put in a couple bids for new projects.

I even cold email a handful of companies I think would like my work that have been on my to-do list forever. Sending cold emails is basically a new record for me. I put it off as long as possible because I hate writing those emails—they seem salesy and weird. I know putting myself out there is a big part of my job, but I still don't like it. I'm supposed to bring in a certain number of clients so I have to. But cold emailing ahead of the deadline … I am … desperate for a distraction.

All this to avoid deciding what to do about Jackson's text.

Do I say something? Ask for clarification?

Send him a message talking up last night as a joke?

That probably wouldn't play very well. Or—I don't know, maybe it would. He's always been laid back and funny. We've never had this much pressure between us.

In the afternoon, I give up trying to work and check his socials. He hasn't unfriended me. Hasn't posted anything there, either.

"Oh, God, Aubree." I bury my face in my hands. He's probably working. It's Monday. Jackson works in finance and it's always busy, even when it's not the craziest part of tax season. He's busy, that's all it is. This isn't a disaster.

We've avoided disaster lots of times. When I first moved back to town, I had a boyfriend. We were going to do the whole long-distance thing and stick it out together. It didn't last longer than three months. My feelings for him cooled once we weren't in the same town. And … my feelings for someone else were heating up.

Jackson.

I felt myself falling for him every Sunday at the football games. I waited for his calls and blushed when I got texts. When Cheryl and I would hang out with him, I tried to be the best, shiniest version of myself, all while I told myself I was being casual. The real me. At some point, those two people got mixed together. I got more comfortable with Jackson.

Too comfortable, to the point that I broke up

with my boyfriend, intending to tell Jackson how I felt.

I was too late. He was already seeing someone else.

What's a girl to do? I told myself it was a crush. You don't bring up a crush to your best friend's brother when he's dating someone else. It was a reasonable crush too. Jackson had treated me well. He'd been kind to me instead of brushing me off as one of his sister's friends, and it would be hard for anyone not to feel something.

And he was sweet. And funny. And he liked flirting with me. But it wasn't … real.

Defeated, I sit back farther in my chair, pulling my legs up and letting the swivel rock me back and forth.

I still feel him all over me from last night. It doesn't matter that I've showered. Doesn't matter that I have fresh clothes and a day of work behind me. The imprints of his kisses are still on my skin. The places where our bodies met are still buzzing from the contact.

When I glance at the clock next, it's five fifteen.

I take my teacup to the sink and wash it. It's probably the most thorough bath the teacup has ever gotten in its life. Work's over. There are no new messages from Jackson on my phone. Nothing laughing off the text I sent him, or asking for a reply.

If he hasn't messaged by six, I'll text him and put myself out of my misery. I can't let this hang over my head all night. Or for the rest of my life. I can't go to the game next weekend feeling all twisted up inside, like I've ruined something.

I haven't, really. The way to think about this is as a nice, onetime thing. We both enjoyed each other, and that's enough. It's a choice to make it awkward with him. I can choose to make it normal instead.

Right?

Although that doesn't explain why I feel this sense of loss inside my chest. This ache for something more.

A knock at the door makes me jump.

I can't deny that it causes a flood of feelings. Embarrassment, because I've been waiting for this knock. Fear, because what if it's not him? And hope —hope that it's Jackson standing on the other side. Who the hell else could it possibly be, though?

I place the teacup in the drying rack as gently as my nerves will allow me and head to the door with even strides so it doesn't sound like I'm running. *It might not be him, anyway.*

I get up on tiptoe to look through the peephole. My heart beats fast and feels skittish. I've never had a crush as strong as this one. Not even when I was a teenager and all my hormones were out of control. The guys in my high school had nothing on Jackson.

Jackson's in the hall outside my apartment, waiting patiently, a bag of Chinese food raised in his hand. "Hey," he calls out. "You hungry?"

JACKSON

I'm not hungry in the least. Even with the scent of Chinese food wafting from the coffee table. The TV plays some sitcom in the background but none of it means a thing.

Not when Aubree doesn't move for the food either. Not when she keeps stealing glances at me and blushing every time our eyes meet.

My nerves work their way through me as I stare at Aubree, needing to tell her exactly how I feel. It's now or never.

I told myself if there was even a hint that she didn't regret last night, that she wanted to be something more, I was going to do it.

And now's my chance.

It's so quiet, my dry swallow is audible. My

cheeks burn with the heat of embarrassment when she stares down at her plate, speechless.

"I loved last night. I've had feelings for you for years." I can't stop now. She has to know. I leave my hand on the coffee table, palm up and she notices. Her gaze moves to it and then back up to mine.

"I didn't know I was that good in bed," she jokes and I laugh, a genuine chuckle to match hers. But I don't back down.

My anxiousness scatters. The relief of knowing she's not running at the thought is all I needed.

Before I can say anything, she scoots closer on the sofa, her warmth immediately evident. "You were pretty good in bed too, if I might add," she teases me, her long lashes fluttering.

My thumb rubs a soothing circle over her knuckles as I debate on the next step.

"Just tell me what to say." I practically beg her like the desperate man I am.

"What?"

"I will say whatever I need to … to get you to say you'll be mine right now," I tell her in all honesty. The subtle shock, the awe that follows, lets me know that she hears me. And that she knows I'm serious.

"I want to be with you. More than friends. I can't go back to being just friends."

"Jackson …" Her hand leaves mine and she tucks it into her lap.

That slight panic of losing her comes back.

"I'll be damned if I lose you, Aubree," I confess, not hiding my desperation. "This isn't some one-night fling. I don't want that."

She whispers the one fear I've had for years that kept me from kissing her, "What if it doesn't work?"

"What if it does?" My answer is immediate and her gaze falls to my lips, then darts back up to me. "I want you. If you want me too, just say yes."

A beat passes. And then another. Too many seconds go by, filling me with an anxiousness until she whispers, "Yes."

That's all I needed for relief to take over and to lean down and capture her lips with mine. I don't even realize what I'm doing until this gentle kiss is over and a soft moan of satisfaction falls from her lips. With her eyes still closed, I take her in and this moment between us.

"I mean it, Aubree," I tell her, then clear my throat and wait for her to peer back at me. My heart hammers but I don't hold back anymore. "I could see you walking down the aisle … I can see all of what I want in the future, happening with you."

Her chest rises with a slow, yet deep inhale at my admission.

"Jackson," she says, merely whispering my name, her longing gaze never leaving mine. With her small hand she fists the fabric of my shirt, taking what's hers as she pulls me down, devouring my lips with hers and letting her hunger take over.

Her soft body presses against mine and she climbs into my lap and all of last night comes back with a force. My cock is hard in an instant and I smile against her kiss as she pushes my shoulders back, easing me onto my back on her sofa.

As she sits up, straddling me and pulling her shirt over her head, I chuckle. "You are so damn good with your words, you know that?"

That sweet feminine laugh I know so well brightens up her face as she reaches behind her, unhooking her bra. It falls easily from her, revealing her supple breasts and rose petal nipples. I can't help the tortured groan that escapes me.

"Was that a word, Jackson?" she says, teasing me as she leans down, her palm resting beside my head. Her hair falls in front of her, obstructing my view. "I'm not sure I–"

In a swift motion, I grip her hips and flip her smart ass over so she's beneath me and I'm on top. Her gasp of surprise is accompanied by her legs wrapping around my hips.

I lean forward, pressing myself into her and rocking my hips.

"You teasing me, Aubree?" I murmur, letting the hint of a threat hang between us. "I think I could find a way to tease you back."

Her lips part with the sexiest fucking inhale I've ever heard in my life.

"Oh yeah," she says in a breathy voice. "I think I'd like that."

"Like?" I cock a brow.

"I think I'd love it if you teased me for the rest of my life, Jackson."

An asymmetric grin pulls at my lips. "Now that's the challenge I've been waiting for."

EPILOGUE

Aubree

One year later

The cheers erupt from every soul in here, including Michelle, who's got the baby in a carrier. The little one wears the cutest pair of baby earmuffs you've ever seen, which is a must for game nights at the bar. Technically she's too young to be allowed in, but this is a small town and even if she's not yet one, she can't miss this make-or-break game to see who's headed to the playoffs.

Just like old times, we're all here in our booth at
The Peanut Bar. Nick and Michelle and baby. Nate
and Anne. Cheryl and me.

The only one missing is Jackson.

Not *missing* missing. Just late. Late for the game
that takes place at the same time every Sunday. My
foot taps erratically wondering where the heck he is.

"He's going to miss the second quarter," I fret to
Cheryl. I'm not exactly worried for him. He's a
grown man and The Peanut Bar is in the same place
as always. We even planned to come here sepa-
rately, me with Cheryl and him with …

Well, nobody. Since we're together. A smile
creeps up to my lips as I check my phone again.
Together, together.

We've been together since the night with the
Chinese food. The awkward Sunday football game
never happened, because it was never awkward. We
simply showed up and announced we were a thing
and ordered everyone a shot to celebrate. I'll never
forget Cheryl's scream and Anne's hug of unadul-
terated joy. *About time* was said a lot that night.

"The first quarter's not over yet." Cheryl pats
my arm with a gleam in her eye. "Relax. Want
another drink?"

"I've barely had any of this one." The IPA
sloshes in my glass as I tilt it.

Because I don't want to have fun without him.

Jackson's easygoing, but I take my time with him seriously. If I'm going to get buzzed at the bar, I want it to be with him standing next to me and ready to take me home.

Fine. I want everything to happen with him standing next to me. It's a huge victory to be with him, in my mind. He represents growing into myself as a woman and taking control of my own life. For once, I didn't shove down my feelings and pretend they were worthless. I acted on them, and now I have the best man I could imagine.

Our team kicks off the ball, and the players rush around the field, arranging and rearranging themselves for the next series. I like when we play defense. Cheryl thinks offense is more exciting, but I like standing up for what you've earned. Plus, there's a chance we catch an interception, which is the most thrilling thing that can happen in football.

The opposing team's quarterback lines up, catches the snap, and throws the ball.

One of our guys jumps into the air, his hands up high. Almost—almost—

He misses.

"Oh, man, that was close."

Nobody else in the bar reacts. I turn to Cheryl to see why not, but she's not looking at me.

She's looking at the man who just walked in through the front door of the bar.

Jackson.

He's not dressed for a football game. No well-worn jeans, no sweatshirt or jersey.

He's in a trim-cut suit that hugs his shoulders just right. A suit I've never seen him in. One that looks expensive as hell.

My mouth waters although my head is wondering if I've slipped and fallen. I could be dreaming right now and I wouldn't want a soul to wake me up. This is more than what he wears to the office. He's taken more care with his appearance, and everybody notices. How could you not? He's all dark hair and blue eyes and wearing a jacket that fits him like he was meant to be on the cover of a magazine.

"Hey, Dani," he calls out although his sharp gaze is pinned on me. "Can you turn the volume down a second?"

I barely glance to the left. The bartender smiles. The volume lowers on the TVs. To my shock, nobody protests. My heart flutters in my chest. *What's happening?*

Jackson strides over to me, eating up the distance too quickly for me to process that this is even real. He gives a wave to all our friends at the bar and everybody else who's come to watch the game. "I want all of you to hear this, okay?"

"What are you doing?" I whisper beneath my breath although he takes my hands in his.

With a nervous smile, he gets down on one knee.

Oh my God.

"Aubree, I've had a crush on you since the first day we met."

My mouth drops open. He did not. I had the crush on him.

Jackson laughs. "I know. I never told you, because I didn't want to scare you off. But now the whole town can hear, and I don't care. I want them all to know how much I love you. I want you to know how much I love you. I want to spend every Sunday with you for the rest of our lives. Will you marry me?"

"Yes," I squeak. I take his face in my hands. "Yes, of course I do."

"Do you want to see the ring first, maybe?"

Laughter fills the bar, and it's so warm and welcoming. That's the sound of my friends being happy for us. Our friends. We didn't have to give any of them up.

I can barely get out the words as I tell him, "I'd marry you without a ring."

Jackson shakes his head and pulls a ring box out of his pocket. He opens it with a flourish. From behind him, Cheryl gasps. "That's way bigger than you said it was!"

"What?" he answers, sheepish and proud and before he can respond, I pull him to his feet and kiss him. Fisting his shirt and desperate to seal the deal. A cheer goes up from all around us. This is what it means to have a good life. This is what it means to be happy. As soon as I'm done kissing Jackson, he slides the ring on my finger and steps out of the way.

"What are you—"

Cheryl throws herself at me, wrapping her arms around my neck. "Do you have any idea how hard that was to keep a secret?" She laughs. "Let me see, let me see." Cheryl takes my hand and looks down at the diamond sparkling on my finger. "It's perfect." Then she tugs her brother back into place at my side. "You're both perfect together. I'm going to give the best maid of honor speech."

"Who said you were going to be—" Jackson begins.

"Oh, stop," I say, cutting him off. Dani turns the game back up on the TVs. "She's going to be my maid of honor. And you're going to be my husband."

He gives me that charming smile that makes everything around us fade to nothing.

"I love you, Aubree."

"I love you too."

Looking for another sexy contemporary romance?
Then snag **Knocking Boots (A Novel)** today!

They were never meant to be together.
Charlie is a bartender with noncommittal
tendencies.
Grace is looking for the opposite. Commitment.
Marriage. A baby.

ABOUT WILLOW WINTERS

Thank you so much for reading my romances. I'm just a stay at home mom and avid reader turned author and I couldn't be happier.
I hope you love my books as much as I do!

More by Willow Winters

Sign up for my Newsletter to get all my romance releases, sales, sneak peeks and a **FREE** Romance, **Burned Promises**

If you prefer *text alerts* so you don't miss any of my new releases, text
US residents: Text WILLOW to 797979
UK residents: Text WWINTERS to 82228

ALSO BY WILLOW WINTERS

Small Town Romance

Tequila Rose Book 1
Autumn Night Whiskey Book 2
He tasted like tequila and the fake name I gave him
was Rose.
Four years ago, I decided to get over one man, by
getting under another. A single night and nothing
more.
Now, with a three-year-old in tow, the man I still
dream about is staring at me from across the street
in the town I grew up in. I don't miss the flash of
recognition, or the heat in his gaze.
The chemistry is still there, even after all these
years.

I just hope the secrets and regrets don't destroy our
second chance before it's even begun.

Tequila Rose World Standalones

A Little Bit Dirty

Kiss Me in this Small Town

Contemporary Romance Standalones

Knocking Boots (A Novel)

They were never meant to be together.
Charlie is a bartender with noncommittal
tendencies.
Grace is looking for the opposite. Commitment.
Marriage. A baby.

Promise Me (A Novel)

She gave him her heart. Back when she thought
they'd always be together.
Now **Hunter** is home and he wants Violet back.

Tell Me To Stay (A Novella)

He devoured her, and she did the same to him.
Until it all fell apart and Sophie ran as far away
from **Madox** as she could.

After all, the two of them were never meant to be together?

Second Chance (A Novella)
No one knows what happened the night that forced them apart. No one can ever know.
But the moment **Nathan** locks his light blue eyes on Harlow again, she is ruined.
She never stood a chance.

Burned Promises (A Novella)
Derek made her a promise. And then he broke it.
That's what happens with your first love.
But Emma didn't expect for Derek to fall back into her life and for her to fall back into his bed.

You Are Mine Series of Duets

You Are My Reason (You Are Mine Duet book 1)
You Are My Hope (You Are Mine Duet book 2)
Mason and Jules emotionally gripping romantic suspense duet.
One look and Jules was tempted; one taste, addicted.
No one is perfect, but that's how it felt to be in Mason's arms.
But will the sins of his past tear them apart?

You Know I Love You
You Know I Need You
Kat says goodbye to the one man she ever loved
even though **Evan** begs her to trust him.
With secrets she couldn't have possibly imagined,
Kat is torn between what's right and what was right
for them.

Tell Me You Want Me
This is Sue's story.

Valetti Crime Family Series:
A HOT mafia series to sink your teeth into.

Dirty Dom
Becca came to pay off a debt, but **Dominic Valetti**
wanted more.
So he did what he's always done, and took what he
wanted.

His Hostage
Elle finds herself in the wrong place at the wrong
time. The mafia doesn't let witnesses simply walk
away.
Regret has a name, and it's **Vincent Valetti**.

Rough Touch

Ava is looking for revenge at any cost so long as she can remember the girl she used to be. But she doesn't expect **Kane** to show up and show her kindness that will break her.

Cuffed Kiss

Tommy Valetti is a thug, a mistake, and everything Tonya needs; the answers to numb the pain of her past.

Bad Boy

Anthony is the hitman for the Valetti familia, and damn good at what he does. They want men to talk, he makes them talk. They want men gone, bang - it's done. It's as simple as that.
Until Catherine.

Those Boys Are Trouble (Valetti Crime Family Collection)

To Be Claimed Saga

A hot tempting series of fated love, lust-filled secrets and the beginnings of an epic war.

Wounded Kiss
Gentle Scars
Primal Lust

Broken Fate
Captive Desire
Under His Reign

Read Willow's sexiest and most talked about
romances in the Merciless World

This Love Hurts Trilogy
This Love Hurts
But I Need You
And I Love You the Most

An epic tale of both betrayal and all-consuming
love...
Marcus, the villain.
Cody Walsh, the FBI agent who knows too much.
And Delilah, the lawyer caught in between.

What I Would do for You (This Love Hurts Trilogy
Collection)

A Kiss to Tell (a standalone novel)
They lived on the same street and went to the same
school, although he was a year ahead. Even so
close, he was untouchable.
Sebastian was bad news and Chloe was the sad girl
who didn't belong.
Then one night changed everything.

Possessive (a standalone novel)
It was never love with **Daniel Cross** and she never
thought it would be. It was only lust from a
distance. Unrequited love maybe.
He's a man Addison could never have, for so many
reasons.

Merciless Saga
Merciless
Heartless
Breathless
Endless

Ruthless, crime family leader **Carter Cross**
should've known Aria would ruin him the moment
he saw her. Given to Carter to start a war; he was
too eager to accept. But what he didn't know was
what Aria would do to him. He didn't know that she
would change everything.

All He'll Ever Be (Merciless Series Collection of all
4 novels)

Irresistible Attraction Trilogy
A Single Glance
A Single Kiss
A Single Touch

Bethany is looking for answers and to find them she needs one of the brothers of an infamous crime family, **Jase Cross**.
Even a sizzling love affair won't stop her from getting what she needs.
But Bethany soon comes to realise Jase will be her downfall, and she's determined to be his just the same.

Irresistible Attraction (A Single Glance Trilogy Collection)

Hard to Love Series
Hard to Love
Desperate to Touch
Tempted to Kiss
Easy to Fall

Eight years ago she ran from him.
Laura should have known he'd come for her. Men like **Seth King** always get what they want.
Laura knows what Seth wants from her, and she knows it comes with a steep price.
However it's a risk both of them will take.

Not My Heart to Break (Hard to Love Series Collection)

Shame On You Series
Tease Me Once
I'll Kiss You Twice
Then You're Mine
Tease me once... I'll kiss you twice.
Declan Cross' story from the Merciless World.

Spin off of the Merciless World

Love the Way Trilogy
Kiss Me
Hold Me
Love Me

With everything I've been through, and the
unfortunate way we met, the last thing I thought I'd
be focused on is the fact that I love the way you
kiss me.

**Extended epilogues to the Merciless World
Novels**
A Kiss To Keep (more of Sebastian and Chloe)
Seductive (more of Daniel and Addison)
Effortless (more of Carter and Aria)
Never to End (more of Seth and Laura)

**Sexy, thrilling with a touch of dark Standalone
Novels**

Broken (Standalone)

Kade is ruthless and cold hearted in the criminal world.

They gave Olivia to him. To break. To do as he'd like.

All because she was in the wrong place at the wrong time. But there are secrets that change everything.

And once he has her, he's never letting her go.

Forget Me Not (Standalone novel)

She loved a boy a long time ago. He helped her escape and she left him behind. Regret followed her every day after.

Jay, the boy she used to know, came back, a man.

With a grip strong enough to keep her close and a look in his eyes that warned her to never dare leave him again.

It's dark and twisted.

But that doesn't make it any less of what it is.

A love story. Our love story.

<u>It's Our Secret</u> (Standalone novel)

It was only a little lie. That's how stories like these get started.

But with every lie Allison tells, **Dean** sees through it.

She didn't know what would happen. But with all

the secrets and lies, she never thought she'd fall for him.

Collections of shorts and novellas

Don't Let Go
A collection of stories including:
Infatuation
Desires in the Night and Keeping Secrets
Bad Boy Next Door

Kisses and Wishes
A collection of holiday stories including:
One Holiday Wish
Collared for Christmas
Stolen Mistletoe Kisses

All I Want is a Kiss (A Holiday short)
Olivia thought fleeting weekends would be enough
and it always was, until the distance threatened to
tear her and **Nicholas** apart for good.

Highest Bidder Series:

Bought
Sold
Owned

Given

From USA Today best selling authors, Willow
Winters and Lauren Landish, comes a sexy and
forbidden series of standalone romances.

Highest Bidder Collection (All four Highest Bidder
Novels)

**Bad Boy Standalones, cowritten with Lauren
Landish:**

Inked
Tempted
Mr. CEO

Three novels featuring sexy powerful heroes.
Three romances that are just as swoon-worthy as
they are tempting.

Simply Irresistible (A Bad Boy Collection)

Forsaken, (A Dark Romance cowritten with B. B.
Hamel)

Grace is stolen and gifted to him; Geo a dominating,
brutal and a cold hearted killer.

However, with each gentle touch and act of
kindness that lures her closer to him, Grace is
finding it impossible to remember why she should
fight him.

Happy reading and best wishes,
Willow xx

CONNECT WITH AMELIA WILDE

Amelia Wilde is a USA TODAY bestselling author of dangerous contemporary romance and loves it a little *too* much. She lives in Michigan with her husband and daughters. She spends most of her time typing furiously on an iPad and appreciating the natural splendor of her home state from where she likes it best: inside.

Need more dangerous romance right now? Read her dark contemporary retelling of the famous Hades & Persephone right now in King of Shadows!

Need more stories like this one in your life? Sign up for her newsletter here and receive access to subscriber-only previews, giveaways, and more!

Follow her on BookBub for new release alerts!

Still can't get enough? Join her reader's group on Facebook and enter the party today!

Made in the USA
Columbia, SC
19 June 2024

36932516R00048